For my Minnesota family and friends
M. M.

Text copyright © 2013 by Megan McDonald
Illustrations copyright © 2013 by G. Brian Karas

First edition 2013

Library of Congress Catalog Card Number 2012947754
ISBN 978-0-7636-5712-3

13 14 15 16 17 18 CCP 10 9 8 7 6 5 4 3 2 1

Printed in Shenzhen, Guangdong, China

This book was typeset in Usherwood.
The illustrations were done in gouache, acrylic, and pencil.

Candlewick Press
99 Dover Street
Somerville, Massachusetts 02144

visit us at www.candlewick.com

Contents

CHAPTER I
Dark Days

Ant looked out the window. Gray clouds. Gray sky. Gray trees. Gray earth. It was the first day of winter.

Ant tuned the radio to KANT 107. "Cold. Rain. Sleet. Snow," said the radio.

Oh, no! *Snow!* Ant did not like cold. Ant did not like freezing rain or slush or sleet or hail. Ant did *not* like winter.

"The Dark Days are here," she said.
Time to hibernate. She would not be
going outside for a very long time.

Ant sighed. She already missed
Honey Bee. At the first sign of winter,
Honey Bee had holed up inside her
house.

Ant and Honey Bee were a pair. A pair of friends. They went together like peanut butter and jelly. Now Ant would not see her friend until spring. But Ant was not ready to go to sleep yet.

"I can have fun all by myself." Ant tried to think of one-person things to do.

Ant read a book.

Ant wrote a poem in her journal.

Ant painted a picture. A picture of

Ant and Honey Bee. It only made her

miss her friend more.

Ant lay on the couch. "Winter gives
me time to think. Thinking is a one-
person thing to do."

Ant stared at the ceiling. Ant thought
and thought. But all she could think
about was Honey Bee.

It was not even lunchtime, and Ant was already out of one-person things to do.

Ding! Her computer! Maybe it was a bee-mail from Honey Bee. No. It was only an ad from Ants R Us.

Ant e-mailed her friend.

Ant waited to hear back. She tapped

her fingers. She played solitaire. She

stared at her computer. Nothing. Not a

word. Maybe Honey Bee was already

asleep for the winter.

Ding! At last, a bee-mail from Honey Bee.

To: Ant @ anthill

Dear Ant,

I am busy. Busy being alone.

Love, HoneyBee :)

Honey Bee was not asleep. Honey Bee was awake. And alone.

Ant had an idea. She put on her puffy coat.

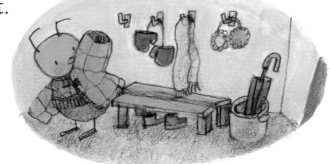

She put on her fluffy scarf and mittens.

She put on her earmuffs and boots.

Outside, it was rainy and complain-y.

Soon it would be snowy and blowy. But

Ant would brave the cold! Ant would

rescue her friend from being all alone.

She dashed through sleet and wind and rain, past Beetle and Fly's house, past Old Man Spider's house, past Cricket's house, all the way to Honey Bee's front door.

CHAPTER 2
EEP OT

A sign on Honey Bee's door said EEP O T.

"Eep Ot?" said Ant. "That sign does not make sense. Maybe it's Spanish. Or French. It must mean 'Come in.'"

Ant pushed open the front door.

Honey Bee was reading the paper. She looked up. "Didn't you get my bee-mail?" she asked.

"Uh-huh," said Ant. "It said you were alone. So I rushed right over."

"Didn't you read my sign?" asked Honey Bee. "It says KEEP OUT."

"I read your sign," said Ant. "It does not say KEEP OUT. It says EEP OT."

"That doesn't even make sense," said Honey Bee.

"That's what I said!" Ant said.

"Never mind," said Honey Bee. "I'm tired. And hungry. And grumpy." Honey Bee sure had her stinger out today.

"I just want to put my feet up and read my paper in peace," Honey Bee told Ant. Honey Bee went back to reading.

"That paper is full of bad news," said Ant. "No wonder you're grumpy."

"You would be, too, if you were the hardest worker bee in the hive," said Honey Bee. "I'm sorry, Ant, but you can't stay. I just want to be alone."

"But you have *all winter* to be alone," said Ant. "Besides, I'm out of one-person things to do."

"I need Peace and Quiet," said Honey Bee.

"I can be quiet," said Ant. "I can be as quiet as a blade of grass in summer. You won't even know I'm here!"

Ant sat and sat. Ant tried to be as quiet as a blade of grass. Being quiet made her antsy.

"Honey Bee? What do you think about when you are all alone?" asked Ant.

"I don't know — because I'm *not* alone."

"Just pretend I'm not here," said Ant.

"I could pretend better if you *weren't* here," said Honey Bee.

"Can't we *do* something?" asked Ant.

"I *am* doing something," said Honey Bee. "I'm doing nothing."

"Nothing isn't something," said Ant. "Let's play a game. Tic-tac-toe?"

"Tic-tac-*NO,*" said Honey Bee.

Ant slumped. Ant harrumphed.

"Okay, I have a game we can play,"

said Honey Bee.

Ant yippeed. "I love games!"

"Let's play the game of Be Quiet.

Whoever talks first loses."

"But —" said Ant. Honey Bee

shushed her.

Ant tried very hard to be quiet. She itched. She twitched.

"I have too many words inside me to hold them all in!" she cried.

"I win," said Honey Bee. Honey Bee went back to her Bad News paper.

Ant looked around the room for something new to do. She saw a basket full of blocks. "Let's build the world's biggest skyscraper!" said Ant. "Taller than the Eiffel Tower!"

"*Non, merci,*" said Honey Bee, which was French for *No, thanks.*

Ant found a tub full of art supplies.
"Let's make the world's biggest Work
of Art! You can be the famous artist
Georgia O'Bee. I'll be Ansel Ant."

"I have a better idea," said Honey
Bee. "You can be Vincent Van Go and
Go Home."

Ant opened a trunk full of costumes.
"Let's play dress-up! You'll tell me I look
very antsome, and I'll say you look
bee-u-tiful."

"I'm too tired to be bee-u-tiful," said Honey Bee. "And too hungry to say anything nice."

"And don't forget too grumpy," Ant added.

Honey Bee closed her eyes. Honey Bee let out a great big YAWWN.

Ant fluffed a pillow and tucked it under her friend's feet. "Honey Bee! I have an idea. Why don't *you* be Queen Bee for a day? I will be the worker bee. I mean worker ant. I will even cook lunch for you. All by myself."

"But you've never cooked anything

before," said Honey Bee.

"How hard can it be?" Ant asked.

"Well, okay," said Honey Bee, "but

don't go into the pantry, because . . .

because there's nothing in there."

Ant went to the kitchen. Ant did

not go into the pantry. Ant opened the

cupboard over the sink.

"Honey, honey, honey," said Ant.

"All you have is honey!"

"Don't touch the honey!" called Honey Bee. "I had to visit two million flowers to make that honey. I need it to get me through the winter."

"I am going to make you something much better than honey," said Ant.

"What could be better than honey?" asked Honey Bee.

"You'll see," said Ant.

"Do you have any bread?" called Ant.

Honey Bee did not answer.

"Never mind," Ant called. "I found some old chips."

"You didn't go into the pantry, did you?"

"No, I did not," answered Ant. "Do you have any peanut butter?"

Honey Bee did not answer.

"I will have to make do without peanut butter," Ant said to herself.

"Then do you have any jelly?" she called.

Honey Bee still did not answer.

Aha! The fridge! Ant looked in the
fridge. *Crumbs!* No jelly! Just *royal* jelly.

Royal jelly was not jelly. Royal jelly

was milk. Honey Bee milk.

Ant did not know if she should pour milk on a sandwich. But the old chips in the two bowls looked lonely all by themselves. So Ant poured some milk on them.

The chips bobbed and floated to the top.

"Lunch is ready," called Ant. "Come and get it!"

CHAPTER 3
Peanut Butter and Jelly

Honey Bee came into the kitchen.

"Ta-da!" Ant pointed to her creation.

Honey Bee looked at the old chips floating in milk. "What is that?" Honey Bee asked.

"My favorite thing in all the world!" said Ant.

"Milk . . . soup?" asked Honey Bee.

"A peanut-butter-and-jelly sandwich!"
said Ant.

Honey Bee did not see any peanut
butter. Honey Bee did not see any jelly.
Honey Bee did not even see any bread. All
she saw were chips swimming in milk.

"It's hard to make a peanut-butter-and-jelly sandwich without peanut butter," said Ant. "You have to use lots of imagination."

"Hmm," said Honey Bee. "Maybe we could dress it up a little?"

"Dress up? Sure!" said Ant. "But what will we use? There's nothing here."

"The cupboard *is* bare," said Honey Bee.

"What a disaster," said Ant. "It's a peanut-butter-and-jelly emergency."

Honey Bee chewed on the problem for a bit.

Honey Bee looked at the milk soup.

Honey Bee looked at Ant.

"I'll be right back," she said. Honey Bee flew from the room. She looked around for a box. She got out a fat marker. She zoomed into the pantry with the box and the marker and shut the door behind her.

Finally, she came back out of the
pantry with the big box that now said:

"But I thought you said there was
nothing in the pantry."

"That's right. Nothing but . . . my
disaster kit!" said Honey Bee.

"Here, let me help!" said Ant.

"It's too heavy for you," said Honey Bee.

"Are you kidding? I can lift fifty times my own weight." Ant took the box and set it down. They opened it. Crackers, chips, and cookies! Raisins and rice cakes! Cereal, spaghetti sauce, and sprinkles!

"Cheese and crackers!" cried Ant.
"There's enough here for a picnic palooza!"

Honey Bee pulled out two pieces of
Beehive Oven Bread.

"What should go on the sandwich first?"
Ant asked.

"Peanut butter," said Honey Bee.

"And Marshmallow Fluff!" said Ant.

"Then raisins," said Honey Bee.
"And maybe some maple syrup."

Ant added goldfish-shaped crackers
and gummy worms.

Honey Bee piled on pita chips,
pretzels, and a pickle.

Ant tossed on tuna fish, taco shells, and trail mix.

"Dried apples!" said Ant.

"Fruit Roll-Ups!" said Honey Bee.

Honey Bee sprinkled on choco chips.

Ant crumbled cookie crumbs on top.

"Ketchup!" said Honey Bee.

"Squeeze cheese!" shouted Ant.

The sandwich grew bigger and bigger.

The sandwich grew higher and higher.

The sandwich grew taller and taller.

"This is the best sandwich ever," said Ant. "Let's eat."

"Something is missing,"

said Honey Bee.

"What could be missing?"

said Ant. "Our sandwich is

as tall as the Eiffel Tower and

has everything in it but the

kitchen sink."

"That's it!" said Honey Bee.

"The kitchen sink?" asked Ant.

"No! *Above* the kitchen sink. HONEY!"

"But you said the honey had to get you through the long winter."

"Well, it *is* winter. It's the *first day* of winter," said Honey Bee. Honey Bee poured honey all over the sandwich. Honey, honey, honey. Gooey, chewy, runny honey.

"Bon appétit!" said Honey Bee, which
is French for *Happy eating!*

"It's very antsome," said Honey Bee.

"It's bee-u-ti-ful," said Ant.

"This sandwich is a Work of Art!"
said Honey Bee.

"This sandwich is fit for a Queen-
Bee-for-a-day," said Ant.

Ant and Honey Bee ate the sandwich.
They sipped and slurped and crunched
and munched their way through the
whole entire Eiffel Tower. They ate
enough to last them all winter long.

"Good to the last crumb," said Ant.
"That was the best peanut-butter-and-
jelly sandwich in all the world."

"There is nothing better than a peanut-butter-and-jelly sandwich on the first day of winter," said Honey Bee. "Pass the royal jelly, please."

Ant looked at the mess they had made. "This kitchen is a disaster area."

"Good thing I remembered my *disaster* kit!" said Honey Bee.

"Yes, it was a very good thing, Honey Bee." Ant's tummy felt full. Her eyes got droopy.

"I'm too tired to wash a dish," said Honey Bee.

"Me, too," said Ant.

Honey Bee yawned. "I'm *so* sleepy."

"Me, too," said Ant.

Honey Bee pointed out the window. "Look. It's starting to snow! Why don't you stay here and we can take a nap?"

"Honey Bee," said Ant, "aren't you glad I decided to EEP OT?"